Mama's Love Language

BY ELISA STAD

ILLUSTRATED BY RY MENSON

PAPERBACK ISBN # – 979-8-9883785-0-1
HARDCOVER ISBN # – 979-8-9883785-1-8
ELECTRONIC ISBN # – 979-8-9883785-2-5
Library of Congress Control Number: 2023919051

Ginger Lotus Press.
Illustrated by Ry Menson.

Publisher's Note: This is a work of fiction. All of the characters, places, and situations portrayed in this book are the products of the author's imagination. Any correlations to real life are purely coincidental.

Printed in the United States of America.

Dedicated with appreciation to Mom,
and love to Ethan, Kennedy, Avery
-ES

My name is Jade. I live in two worlds.
My mama is Chinese and my dad
is American.

Who am I?

This is my dad.

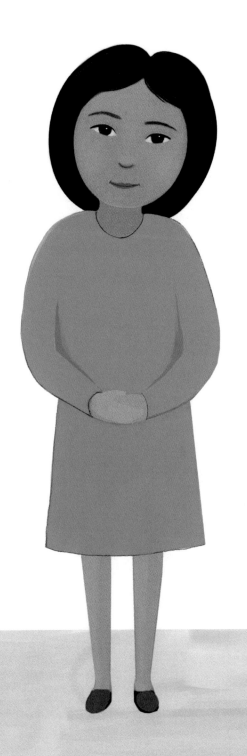

This is my mama.

My dad always hugs me.
My mama never does.
All the other parents at
school hug their kids.

At the grocery store, the cashier doesn't understand her.

At school, we work on our self-portraits.
I draw myself with blonde hair, blue eyes,
and fair skin like my dad.

The mirror shows a different person,
but that's not who I want to be.
I don't match the other kids in my class.

Later that day, at dinner time,
my mama insists, "You must eat
every grain of rice!"

"I'm not eating that," I exclaim.
"I'm not Chinese!"

"You are Chinese!"
my mama yells
and I run to my
room in tears.

Later that evening, my dad checks in on me.

"I heard you did not want to eat your dinner. Hainan chicken rice is your favorite," he says.

"I eat hamburgers like everyone else. I'm American," I sniffle. "Mama doesn't understand me like you do."

"You are both – American and Chinese – as you are made up of *both* your mother and me."

I smell the
healing aroma of
ginger, green onions, and
chicken broth. My tummy rumbles.

In front of me is the dish I have loved
for as long as I can remember.
Steamed chicken, scallions, Gailan
broccoli, broth, and fragrant ginger rice.

"This dish is from Hainan
where your grandparents,
Popo and Gong Gong, were
from," explains my mama.
"Your great-grandparents fled from
China to Vietnam during the war."

I wonder about fighting, danger, and
escape. It makes my heart pound.

"Jay..."
Why can't my mama say my name correctly? I'm frustrated.
"I didn't get a childhood like yours as Popo made me stop attending school to work and support the family," Mama sighs.

I imagine my mama's life without the chance to study and learn like me. I feel uneasy that I had no idea about my mama before me. I want to know more.

"I had to help my mama raise my brothers and sisters in a tiny apartment, and we sometimes didn't have any food to eat," Mama looks past me with sadness in her eyes. "That is why I always make sure you don't waste food and focus on school."

"Your mom didn't speak English when she came to this country," Dad says. "She now speaks five languages fluently — English, Vietnamese, Mandarin, Cantonese, and Hainanese. I love that your mom always cares for family and opens my life to new cultures. I'm fortunate she immigrated here after the war."

And I would not be here if it weren't for my parents. My mama wants a better life for me and I realize how strong my mama had to be. She makes me want to grow and appreciate my life as a student and daughter.

I sip the chicken broth and
I feel the warmth from my lips
to my heart to my belly.
I take a deep breath.

My mama shows love in her own way. Cooking homemade meals. Making sure I do my schoolwork. Caring for me when I don't feel well.

My mama doesn't hug me or say I love you, but when she does all these caring things for me, I feel her love wrap around me like a warm blanket.

The next morning at school, we finish our self-portraits. I look into the mirror and then grab the brown and black pencils to finish mine.

I realize my family is strong and different, and that's special.

I am thankful for my mama's love language. I realize my family is strong and different, which makes me proud to be Jade, or to my mama, "Jay."